NICKELODEON

The BACKYARDIGANS

To the Center of the Earth!

adapted by Catherine Lukas
illustrated by
Jason Fruchter and Aka Chikasawa

SIMON SPOTLIGHT/NICKELODEON
New York   London   Toronto   Sydney

Based on the TV series *Nick Jr. The Backyardigans*™ as seen on Nick Jr.®

 SIMON SPOTLIGHT
An imprint of Simon & Schuster Children's Publishing Division
1230 Avenue of the Americas, New York, New York 10020
© 2009 Viacom International Inc. All rights reserved. NICK JR.,
Nick Jr. The Backyardigans, and all related titles, logos, and characters
are trademarks of Viacom International Inc. NELVANA™ Nelvana Limited.
CORUS™ Corus Entertainment Inc. All rights reserved.
All rights reserved, including the right of reproduction in whole or in part in any form.
SIMON SPOTLIGHT and colophon are registered trademarks of Simon & Schuster, Inc.
Manufactured in the United States of America
10 9 8 7 6 5 4 3
ISBN-13: 978-1-4169-7094-1
ISBN-10: 1-4169-7094-0

"Oh, no! I dropped my lucky penny!" said Tyrone.

"Well you are in luck, my lad," said a voice behind him. "I am Professor Uniqua, the world-famous inventor!"

"And I am Professor Pablo!" said another voice. "Our inventions can do anything! We will help you find your penny!"

"There is only one place your penny could have gone," said Professor Uniqua.

"Are you ready to go?"

"Go where?" asked Tyrone worriedly.

"To the Center of the Earth!" said Professor Pablo.

"And to get there," said Professor Uniqua, "we will have to dig, using one of our amazing inventions."

"Can't I just use this shovel to dig for my penny?" asked Tyrone.

"Poppycock!" said Pablo.

"Balderdash!" said Uniqua. "We will use—the Rocket Drill!"

"We need this big thing to get a penny out of the ground?" asked Tyrone.

"Yes, along with a few other inventions, which we'll pack in this box," said Professor Pablo. "Now hop in! It's a long way to the Center of the Earth."

They all climbed into the Rocket Drill. Then Professor Uniqua pressed a button and . . . BLASTOFF!

They drilled through soil and roots and rocks and mud—and even a layer of lost mittens.

Just after they had drilled through
another layer of rock, Tyrone said,
"Why does it feel like we're falling?"
"Because," said Professor Uniqua,
"we *are* falling. Uh-oh."

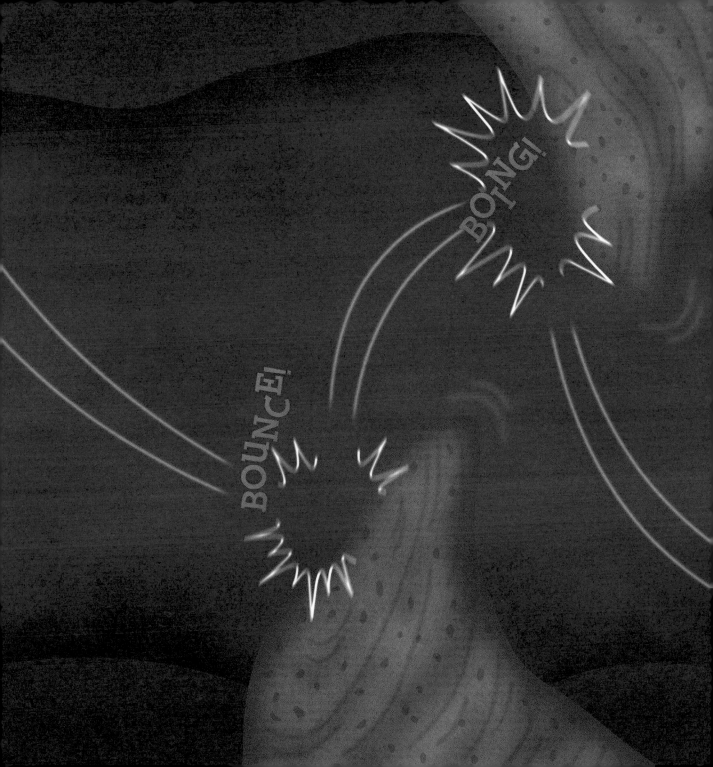

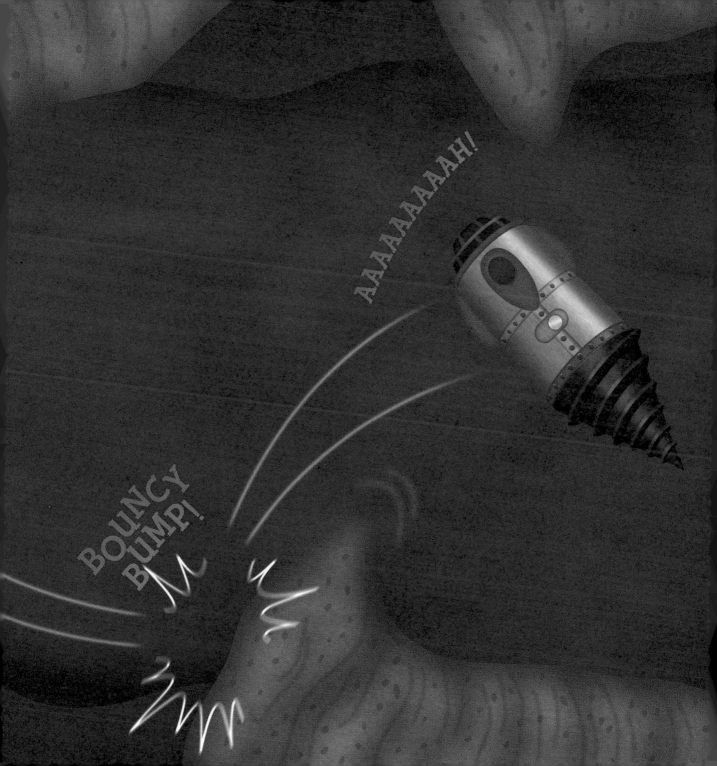

"Oof!" said all three together as the Rocket Drill bounced to a stop. "We seem to have landed on some bouncy surface," said Professor Uniqua. "But we do not seem to be quite at the Center of the Earth." "Look!" shouted Tyrone. "There's my penny! I think I can grab it!"

"Poppycock," said Professor Pablo.

"Balderdash," said Professor Uniqua. "Use an invention instead. See? I will use this remote control to send the Grab-o-Copter over. Watch as I grab the penny like this . . . and then . . . oops."

"My penny!" shouted Tyrone. "It's gone! I knew I should have just picked it up the normal way!"

"Poppycock," said Professor Pablo. "Inventions are always the best way."

"It's fallen farther down," said Professor Uniqua. "Let's get back into the Rocket Drill and keep going toward the Center of the Earth!"

They all leapt in. The professors worked the controls, and the drill began to spin. Down they went. The Rocket Drill crashed through another layer, and then . . .

The Rocket Drill slipped and slid and finally came to a stop in a place filled with sparkling diamonds.

"Look! My penny!" shouted Tyrone. He stumbled across the slippery diamonds until he was standing beneath the penny, which had landed on top of a pointy place. "If I just give this pointy thing a push, the penny should fall into my hand."

"Poppycock!" said Pablo.
"Balderdash!" said Uniqua. "This calls for another invention. Professor Pablo, use these Vacuu-Shoes to climb up and get the penny."

But just as Professor Pablo was nearly about to reach it, the penny fell off and rolled down another hole.

"My penny!" shouted Tyrone.

Tyrone, Uniqua, and Pablo climbed back into the Rocket Drill. They passed through another layer and then landed with a splash in a lake. The Rocket Drill bobbed to the surface.

"I believe we have reached the Center of the Earth!" said Professor Uniqua.

"And look!" said Tyrone, pointing. "There's my penny! It's right next to that sleeping dinosaur!"

"Dinosaur?" all three said together.

"We need to build a quick invention that can pick up that penny," whispered Pablo, rummaging around in the invention-gadget box.

"We can call this . . . Extendo-Arm," whispered Uniqua. "I hope it works."

The Extendo-Arm did grab the penny. But as Uniqua was reeling it in, the Arm swung out and bonked the dinosaur on the head. The penny sailed through the air. Tyrone caught it.

The dinosaur opened its eyes.

"Uh-oh," said Professor Pablo.

"Run!" yelled Uniqua. They turned toward the Rocket Drill just in time to see it sink below the surface of the lake.

"The dinosaur is going to get us!" yelled Pablo.

"Balderdash," said Tyrone calmly.

"Huh?" said the other two, turning around to stare at Tyrone.

"I got my lucky penny back," said Tyrone. He held up his penny so the dinosaur could see it, and then threw his lucky penny as far as he could.

The dinosaur raced away and returned with the penny, which it dropped at Tyrone's feet.

"It's a *friendly* dinosaur!" said Uniqua. "It's playing fetch!"

"If it's so friendly," said Pablo, "why is it growling?"
"That was my stomach," said Uniqua. "I'm hungry!"
"Oh, well in that case," said Tyrone, "let's go to my house and have a snack."

And that's just what they did.